# Blue Sky

# Dark Heart

## Chiesa Irwin

Published by Azurete Press 2009
Azurete Press
P.O. Box 2345
Townsville Post Office
Townsville QLD 4810
Phone: (07) 4779 7584

Cover Design and Typeset by BookPOD
Printed and bound in Australia by BookPOD

National Library of Australia Cataloguing-in-Publication entry

Author:         Irwin, Chiesa.

Title:          Blue sky dark heart / Chiesa Irwin.

Edition:        1st ed.

ISBN:           9780646522166 (pbk.)

ISBN:           9780987213556 (ebook)

Dewey Number:   A821.3

*FOR JIMMY GORDON,*
*a good man on the fighting line.*

PRIVATE JAMES HEATHER GORDON VC
2/31ST AUSTRALIAN INFANTRY BATTALION A.I.F.

PLACE: "GREENHILL" NEAR D'JEZZINE, SYRIA
TIME: THE NIGHT OF 10 JULY 1941

THE ADVANCE OF PRIVATE GORDON'S COMPANY WAS HELD UP BY
INTENSE MACHINE GUN FIRE AND SUFFERED SERIOUS CASUALTIES.
PRIVATE GORDON CHARGED THE OFFENDING POST FROM THE
FRONT AND KILLED THE FOUR MACHINE-GUNNERS WITH THE
BAYONET. HIS ACTION DEMORALISED THE ENEMY IN THIS
SECTION WHICH HIS COMPANY THEN OCCUPIED.
FOR THIS ACTION HE WAS AWARDED THE VICTORIA CROSS.

# Contents

Chiesa Irwin

# The Operator

In the beginning he was an amorous man who enjoyed the company of women. Work weeks spent with other male military members left him craving females. He observed them in all their different ways: the quiet types who would squeak a 'Hello' at him and then cast their eyes down. The exhibitionists loud ones, out on a Saturday night with their girl friends, raucous, sexy, bursting into loud laughter, sassing men from the security of their numbers, piling into a cab for the ride home screeching like monkeys, stumbling out of the cab to lift their skirts to pee in the gutter. Their uninhibitedness overwhelmed him. They were like exotic pets he couldn't afford to own so he watched.

He was drawn to the older ones, likening them to his wife of twenty years; flowers he could open and count the petals of their lives. He was fond of his wife and believed that in giving her pleasure he was fulfilling one of his life's goals. They were paying off a house so they were bound emotionally, physically and financially. He did not consider it a burden.

The military women bothered him a bit so he tried friendly tactics to understand them. He was uncomfortable around them on the training grounds: how could they be trained to kill. It was an ongoing debate he voiced to himself.

To fulfill the requirements for a promotion he accepted a posting that was far away from family obligations. When he arrived at the new military base he had that harassed, stressed look that men wear when mortgage payments, car loans and children's education expenses etch lines of worry across their faces. The advantage of being away from his family provided him with time to study photography and play his favorite sports. On his weekends off he was up early, for him this was the best time of day. He would bike to the old derelict piers and photo the rotting wood; some of the old wooden stumps had metal bands around them and when lit up by the early sun they glowed. The brass was covered with verdigris which dazzled colors through the lens. These pictures were his favorites but he could ruthlessly delete the ones he didn't like. The camera was a key that opened conversations and he spoke to anyone who showed an interest in his art.

His looks were average, tall and lean; he had reached that time of his life where his hair was starting to grey and thin; carrying no fat on his body had kept him young looking and he was pleased that he didn't have the bulky abdomen that most men of his age had developed. He wore glasses, no fancy frames, plain and comfortable they gave him a pleasant look. He looked after his teeth, when others needed a strong cup of coffee to start their day he used a good toothpaste to get it going. He felt his teeth were a hindrance to his appearance, although not a vain man he would have preferred strong white teeth; his were soft and discoloured but he was shy about asking the dentist for a better appearance. Smiling came naturally to him and he hoped that people wouldn't notice them. He considered himself an average bloke not afraid of hard work, enjoyed a cold beer on a hot day and watched footy when he could but it was always women he gravitated to. He had no rating system for them as he felt this was putting them at a disadvantage and he disliked it when other men used a point system for judging women. They were missing out on the good things women offered to the world. Women made his life comfortable but living with the distance from his wife he found himself describing her as his 'partner'. The miles between them had changed her role, she morphed into a modern companion, a partner to visit every three months, similar to an obligation or an X put on a calendar. She called frequently on his mobile phone and it annoyed him to be so reminded of his role as a husband and provider. He wanted freedom not from her but with her and that concept clouded his usually clear vision.

It was an ANZAC day and he was feeling adventurous, up early with his military mates they attended a dawn service, took part in a gunfire breakfast and then they headed to the local RSL where they played two-up with some women from Canada. After that they went into town stopping at various places for drinks. He wanted to feel how far he could push it so he called a woman he knew and spent the night with her. It was a first for him and he felt both ashamed and exhilarated. It opened a part of his life that he had only glimpsed, like figures in an obscure shadow. He wondered if he had hallucinated it. In the days after he avoided the woman and did not acknowledge their tryst but thought of her as the rope that tethered him to the pier and snapping gave him freedom.

He felt women in a different way. Aware of his sexuality he was constantly aroused. Now he thought of himself as a horny man who had ratcheted it up a few notches. He started to sleep with different women and was consumed by guilt afterwards. His needs amazed him, engulfing like a flame that could not be doused; he had a taste for it now. He radiated heat like a sun spot. To compensate he spent more time with men, listening to their stories, talking seriously, making jokes, now he laughed a lot and played down his serious nature. He wanted to be in the company of people; the solitary loner wrapped in his thoughts was evolving into a creature he didn't recognize. Decisions were on him, it was the cross roads of his life and what ever direction he went he clung to his judgment. There was no going back. The future was a book to be read and women were the book marks.

Not accepting the promotional posting he returned to his home and wife. The familiar routine he had enjoyed with her felt stale, frayed around the edges. She had aged a bit but he felt young and eager. Holding her in his arms gave him no comfort, he stopped loving her.    The exotic animals in the jungle of his mind called like music from a planet that held him in a gravitational pull.    He yielded to their song.

# Farewell Tarragona

History relates that Tarragona fell on 1642; the Spanish Wild Geese fought and died there, countries away from their homeland. Strange brogues and accents of the dying men echoed in the dry, dusty roads and fields. Few graves remain to mark their presence. Tarragona fell a second time on January 14, 1939 in the Civil War that was Spain. For 3 years the conflict raged; people who were caught on the 'wrong' side were killed for being there. It was a war of ideologies, misunderstood by the outside world and interpreted by individuals for their own needs. Men from all nations fought in it, some for an idea, a dream picture of the hidden Spain as a land of mystery, beautiful women, bull fights, macho, lusty, a place to be young and headstrong.

General Franco emerged the winner, a dictator less colourful then his contemporaries. A man who quietly signed execution documents while drinking demitasse cups of coffee laced with brandy. His death was unromantic; he lived, he killed, he died. It happened quietly, no flashy bravado, no bund meetings in beer halls. Like all tyrants the grave paid the last respects.

What happened to the men who fought there? Some true romantic souls stayed on, others had caught the wander sickness and drifted through countries like colourful ghosts. The remaining ones returned to their homelands changed by the travels, their souls corrupted by the war. What could their life be when they returned home to mom and dad? Trapped in uneventful jobs and dutiful marriages they remembered the foreign land in dreams. Haunted by memories; their dreams vivid with blood. Waking and still bemused by their memories they would turn to their wives and ask, 'Were you there'?

A young Australian on a quest for adventure went to fight in the civil war. He was vaguely aware of what was happening. The only war memories he had came from his granddad, stories of the Great War and the mates he made and the ones who died. This young man left his shared tent and was walking to the port of Tarragona; one of the pommie lads told him it was a magic place filled with beautiful women. On brief excursions into town he noticed the women seemed to be cloistered between male family members or chaperones. He had stopped at a small market stall and bought oranges. The woman who served him didn't look into his face. All the 'beautiful women' were rumors. On the walk to Tarragona he saw women working in the fields, darkened by the sun, shriveled and hunched over. They waved to him and smiled showing toothless mouths and faces lined with wrinkles that held dirt; naked children played in the dust. It disgusted him to think that he was fighting for these semi-wild poor savages.

It was a long walk under a hot sun until something green showed in the distance and cutting through a field he came upon a small orange grove that glistened like a jewel; there were twelve orange trees planted in rows of threes. They were evenly spaced, no weeds grew among them, and the leaves looked like they had been polished; a small dry stone wall held the rocks that had been cleared from the field. It was a marvel of symmetry. As he moved closer he heard someone call out and he saw an old man running towards him brandishing a hoe. He stopped, held out his hands and said in Spanish...I mean no harm'. The old man stopped and looked at him. He tried out all his best Spanish to explain how beautiful the trees were. The old man took a knife from his pant's pocket and cut off an orange and gave it to him. Gesturing to him he walked back to a hut that was more of a hovel   It barely stood, it was so weather beaten. A mangy rheumatic dog greeted them and with orange juice as sweet as honey dripping from his chin he was invited in. It was dark, one room with a rammed earth floor. A sagging bed and a few utensils were scattered about. A large object was on the bed covered with a bright cloth. He wondered what it was. The old man lead him out and around to the back of the hut where a few broken chairs and an old table with a candle on it were positioned in shade from an old tree. Two wooden crosses were placed into the ground behind the tree. The old man explained they were the graves of his wife and child. The crosses looked ancient.

Someone called out and coming up the side of the orange grove was another old codger. The Australian introduced himself. He drew a map of the world in the dirt and showed them where he was from. They were awestruck that he had come from so far away. He tried to explain Australia to them, when he reached the part about the bushrangers he sang an old bush ballad, 'The Back Block Shearer', and then his granddad's favorite, 'The Morning of the Fray', about the bushranger Frank Gardiner. His grand-dad had toiled at forge and anvil for as long as he knew him, the old man was always singing and when he launched into the 'Fray' song he knew it was all going alright. The two old peasants were laughing and his host went into the hut and brought out a gui-tar and an old squeeze box. The guitar was beautiful, fashioned from dark wood with inlaid mother-of-pearl. The old man told him it came from Portugal then he started to play, his mate took up the squeeze box and they sang their songs. Sometime during the night an orange wine was offered and the young aussie fell asleep on the cold earth under the stars with his head throbbing. In the morning he pointed north and said Tarragona; the old man walked with him part of the way and then went to the grove to tend the trees.

Tarragona was astir; lots of soldiers about, some on horses others in trucks; many were marching in ragged groups bullied on by sergeants, all were wearing the same drab uniform with a cloth hat that sat straight up on the head. He spent the day there, at night he paid an innkeeper a few coins and slept in the stable. It was during the night that the soldiers left. The sky was a brilliant blue when he woke; everything was quiet. Old men sat on wooden steps in front of stores and stared at him as he passed by. He washed in a fountain and wondered where all the beautiful women were. He hadn't seen any.

Back to the tents, he thought, and started the walk back the way he had come. It was the black birds circling in the sky that gave the hint of danger as he neared the orange grove. The trees had been destroyed, they lay like mangled wreckage. The old mate was cradling the body of his host who was dead, beaten to death with a shovel. The old dog's body lay twisted among the trees. He told the aussie how the soldiers had come and destroyed the trees, the old man had died defending his orange trees. The blood on his body was attracting flies so the young man took the bloody shovel and dug a grave for the man and the dog. The old man knelt by the side of the grave and the aussie walked back to his company.

When Madrid surrendered to General Francisco Franco he was watching the victory parade. It had all turned to dust for him and he wondered which of the soldiers had killed the old man. He made plans to return to Australia and in the future when ever he talked about the time he fought in the Spanish civil war he called it 'The Madness'.

On his return this man obtained employment with the local council that was turning swampland into housing estates. In the coming years he became a father and an uncle but still carried the hidden pictures of Spain in his mind and gave the streets in one of the new areas Spanish names that read like a litany of the battles. He must have experienced great love there to be able to scatter the Spanish names on a small map that only he traveled. I think of this person as someone I would have liked to know.

My family owned a house on Tarragona street; highset on a corner block with a pool. Over the years I had many visits there, in my secret heart the house was mine. It was my fancy, my longing. Mentally I re-painted rooms, ripped up the old carpet and polished the floor boards, hung my pictures on the walls, obliterating all traces of my family. When they re-located I was allowed to rent the house. I thought it would be for many years. I made the garden mine, planted trees, shrubs, flowers and bulbs. There were two large mature trees in the yard, a cassia and a poinciana. For generations currawongs and magpies nested in them, bringing their fledglings down to the buffalo grass twice a year. In the arvo rainbow lorikeets would roost in the trees and refresh themselves in the water containers I put out. At night the possums would wake in the palm trees and descend to the cool grass. For me it was a small patch of Paradise. Suddenly my family sold it. I saw it coming but not with such alacrity.

I moved to a grubby maisonette with a shabby garden. I went back for visits and the last time I was there I walked thru the garden, watering plants for the last time. I cupped flowers in my hands and marveled at the staghorn ferns that had circled the ponciana tree. The buffalo grass was the colour of ripe emeralds due to all the rain. It had never been so lush, going shoeless was like walking on carpet. Walking around the pool I was overcome with a desolate feeling of loss. What I thought was mine had never been. My fantasy blew away in the arvo winds.

Where I am staying now is a disappointment, it will never be mine and I don't want it. I share a common driveway with neighbors, people who are modern border-line stupid. No jobs, no cars, no license to even drive one; a crying child. Welfare with 2 mobile phones. They tolerate me, I am kind to them. The world turned and left me in a parallel orbit. I can look but can't feel this place where I am.

Trying to make something better than what it is I dig weeds out of the lawn, plant shrubs, put seed out for the birds. I try not to remember the house on Tarragona street. When I do I focus on the person who named it; a man who traveled to a far away country, fought in battles, loved women, returned home. The sky is blue here but he and I see a different shade.

Chiesa Irwin

# Gold

The man loved beer. Anyway it came, in a tall glass with droplets of moisture streaming down the side, from a cold tinny with the whooshing sound it made when opened, in a stubby bottle that was frosty to the touch. Panic would quicken his thoughts when the beer fridge started to empty. The brew tasted better when there was a good quantity of it. When it was down to the last shelf thoughts of car accidents, having to work back, unforeseen emergencies, even thoughts of death were insignificant when compared with the crushing anxiety of not being able to replenish the supply. When his brother lived with him they were linked in the ritual of buying and storing. The cartons of beer were always bought at the same bottle shop in the local hotel. He bought it cold not minding that it cost more. There was a beer towel in the back of his ute and the cartons would be placed on it such a way that with a turn of his head he could see them. His brother would be waiting for him and together they would unload the cargo silently and thoroughly. They only talked when the first one was cracked. They would sit like friends and reminisce about their travels and events of the long time past. He hated his brother in the present but it was handy to have him share the rent and sometimes he was tolerable in the blurred outline of his world where the beer softened the edges and people overlapped so that at times he couldn't remember whom he was thinking of.

Working as a labourer the day started early, he was on-site before sun up and worked through the late afternoon. In his early fifties he still had the hard compact body needed for work but he noticed there was a slight spread across his middle and he was developing two bald spots on his head, one at the back and the other on the top. He wasn't a vain man but baldness worried him, he remembered his uncles combing long strands of hair from over their ears across their bald heads. He didn't know his father who died when he was an infant. His relatives said that he inherited his bad temper from him. He didn't understand his temper and did nothing to try and ease it. It was a presence that shadowed him and jumped like a fist at all he hated; sports figures, indigenous people, work mates, tv presenters and it seemed anyone who earned a big salary. He raged against them with spoken obscenities and murderous intent. His vortex of violent emotions had cost him jobs so that in middle age it was still hard yakka and he would probably die with his work boots on. His violent temper had ruined all the relationships with the women in his life. The last one had left silently and he still wondered why she went.

On weeknights he went to bed early, exhausted from fatigue and the beers. When he'd return from work the first two he'd drink would pour down his throat with hardly a taste. Then it turned serious, he would stare at the golden liquid as if it contained the secret of life and for him it did. On weekends he would start drinking at eleven am and the concession he made to the early start was that he drank slower and would finish in the late evening. It was pleasant and rosy but sometimes his thoughts were dire and remorseful, anger would rise like bile in his throat. Thoughts, like demons, would come unbidden and he would fill with rancor at imagined slights and unfounded jealousies. Then it would pass and once more he would drown in the golden depths and dancing bubbles. He'd remember his early years in the Air Force and how much he hated it but he was torn by the thought that if he had stayed in his life would be better. He always wondered what it would have been like to accept the discipline, follow the rules and emerge a better person. Then it was time for another beer.

His solitary drinking at home had been a slow adaptation. As a young man his life had revolved around the local hotels and pubs where he and his mates would spend days and nights drinking and then stumble into that stupor that enabled him to sleep on any surface. The best time of his drinking career happened when he matured into a drinker who would spend days drinking in the hot, smoky, smelly atmosphere of his favorite pub. He reveled in the socialization of his drinking mates and as he stood at their table he was close to happiness.  He would stop at the other tables on the way to the gent's room and exchange pleasantries and greetings.  He marveled at the women who could drink their old men out the door and still keep an argument going.  Somewhere in that phase of his public drinking his mates stories became repetitive, they aged.  They annoyed him with their hair loss and health problems.  He was arguing with the men who had been his best friends.  Now he drank at home with the ghosts of his younger years.

He would try to stay up late on weekend nights, catching up on news and sports on tv.  His favorite shows were the black and white war documentaries.  They were shown late and he'd nap while waiting for them to start.  He would wake up to Adolf Hitler and his millions of minions in grainy drab absence of colour.  He believed that there was no colour in the Nazi world, that it only happened when Hollywood started to make war movies. There was der Fuhrer, the great jackboot of all times, with that impossible moustache and limp hair.  He had a theory about Hitler and in his young years in the pubs he would speculate to his mates that Hitler would have been a sweeter person if only he drank.  If he had 'just bent the elbow' a little bit all those people would not have been killed.  As he grew older his theory took on dogma, his belief so strong that he would talk to the dead screen image.  Hitler, in shorts, pictured at his summerhouse with a Tyrolean milkmaid and a background of black and white flowers.  What the dictator needed was beer in a stein with pictures of mountains on it's side and foreign lettering around the rim.

He needed to loosen up at an Oktoberfest and put a bit of vomit on his boots. The Fuhrer is waving to the crowds, swaying back and forth in song; calling to his friend who sees him through an alcoholic glow. His disciple is crying, the intense blue of his younger eyes has faded to a tired washed denim that he doesn't want to see and while he stumbles into bed his tears, like his temper, are not understood. Before passing into sleep he wonders if the Fuhrer would like a cold draught beer before he starts the invasions.

# The Irish Captain

When the military plane arrived in Townsville he was glad to be off it. It was no luxury ride just hard plastic benches along the side; the cargo covered in webbing was stacked in the back with loose gear rolling around the floor. An empty tin of drink ping-ponged from wall to wall. He and the Major reviewed training schedules, dates and the deployment of men into separate groups. Most of the trip was flown over water and when the Townsville coast appeared the plane came in low showing the fabric of the country. Palm trees everywhere reminded him of his base in Borneo. It was still a hot dry summer in Townsville with the smell of bushfires blown on the wind. The military airport proportioned half of the space to commercial carriers and he considered the irony of the scene; travelers jetting off for world trips next to war birds carrying death ordnance. They weren't met so he and the Major shared a taxi to the barracks, their headquarters for the next three months. He settled his gear into a room and armed with a base map he found the mess. One of the last in, he ate in solitary. It was a functional mess, clean and ordinary. One of the civilian staff cleaning the tables greeted him. The army cooks were in a hurry to break down the point so he ate quickly.

Walking around the base he felt the atmosphere of a Sunday night, buildings were isolated in spot lights, the vehicle compounds were well lit, music, conversation and curses coming from the accommodation units. There was a desperate lonely feel to the place. Sunday night was the let-down time. Friday and Saturday nights brought the excitement of being out on the town with the mates, the drinking, the chicks and the fighting. It all dissolved into the suicidal psychosis of the week's end. The men faced with the start of another work week sunk their last beer and sweated it out. He heard arguments, disputes, break ups, mobile phone tones, porn on the lap tops, clothes still spinning in the dryers. He missed his base, the familiar faces, the odors of the jungle night, the bird calls as they settled to roost, the barking of the chit-chats. Here the humidity and heat of this semi-dry tropical place settled around him like a dense cloud. He heard animals, maybe snakes, in the under brush. On the map there were notations of dingo sightings and outside one of the messes was a sign that said not to feed them. He returned to his room and sleep came quickly. Over the next two days the soldiers he would be training arrived along with all the necessary situations that evolved with deployment. The transport vehicles were the easy part, sorting out the confident drivers required tact as many of them wanted to drive.   Picking the best they loaded up and were on the way to High Range.   If he was home in Ireland or England it would be called 'Top End', here in the Townsville bush ' High Range' was inadequate  to describe the terrain they were driving into.   It was a rugged mountain with the truck's engines rapping out a cadence as they climbed.   They followed the Aussies who were also training and his convoy of eager, happy foreign soldiers on a training sortie were up for it.   He settled into a feeling of repose and thought about his life.

He had always been at war.   Growing up Catholic in Belfast had cemented that into his life.   He and his mates roamed the streets like a pack of feral dogs; they took orders from his Aunt Minnie who had raised him.   She was known to the Protestants as the Terror of Falls road and to the Catholics as the Bogside Witch;  she had taught them how to fight.   Armed with Molotov cocktails,  cricket bats and garbage can lids they did much damage.   The Orange lads learned to fight back and there were pitched battles fought out in abandoned lots and alleys.   Whatever the causalities they were always up for the next go.   He was getting the feel for it when caught by a group of British soldiers. Cruising at them when they threw him into the back of a truck he fought like a wild animal.   They forced him to the floor and pined him with their boots.   Arriving at a dark compound he was hauled out of the truck, the first punch took out his teeth. Blood flowed from his ears and nose; they took turns, he was passed from soldier to soldier like a rotating punching bag; he was beaten almost to the edge of death.   When he regained consciousness  he was nude and unable to move.   A few people were standing around him, no one spoke.   An old bloke got him a skivvy and pants, sat him up and dressed him, loaded him into a wheelbarrow and pushed him to his Aunt's house.

He was a long time recovering.   Lying on a pallet in the parlor all he could see was people's legs.   Aunt Minnie would kneel down and say...Johnnie can ye hear me ?   All he could do was shake his head.   When he was able to get around he was treated like an outcast, no place was set for him at the table, it was a shame to them that he had survived, a martyr was better than a broken youth; no glory in that.   He left his Aunt's and drifted along the streets, his gang had been broken up and their moms cursed him.   He went to the church and the old priest told him it was either prison or the army for him.   There was a group of lads queued at an army recruiting station, he joined them and a new life settled around him like a glove.

He was trained to the limit and he proved to them that he could take it.   Nourished, clothed, paid, given teeth; he did courses, hungry for knowledge, eager for the hunt.   A zealot in thrall to war, uniformed for Queen and country.   He enjoyed this life and earned the title of Captain.   There was steel in him wired in an abrupt manner; a harshness to his speech.   No one wanted to be on the receiving end of his wrath.   He was a modern warrior in a world of barracks, rules and regulations led by men with calm eyes that hid rage.

He weathered with the years.   The tattoos on his arms faded to dark lines,  his intense blue eyes turned dull, he retained thick dark hair with a bit of grey at the temples. His body stayed lean and taut, he didn't feel aged. Affairs with women had been disappointments; he no longer sought them out. Through the years he invested in farming properties in England which were managed well. It was always amazement when he studied his portfolio to realize how wealthy he had become.

He was jarred awake when the trucks came to an abrupt halt. A large tree lay across the road, it had come loose with the parched earth still packed around its roots. It had taken a lightening hit and lay there like a diseased animal. It was a chance for everyone to get out of the trucks; an all-terrain vehicle with a double winch was brought forward and they all watched as the tree was dragged to the roadside. Then it was back in the trucks and the serious training begun. His men knew the routine and got into it. The bivouacked among a few gum trees but most of the land was cleared so they transported their gear to where the Australians were setting up equipment. It was hard slog in the heat and wind. The air currents rushed passed them burning their skin. Most of the area had been bushfired, the burnt trees showing tiny green leaves of new growth. Stepping under an out cropping of bush rock he removed his beret and a large tree spider sliding down the rocks landed on his head; it was like wearing a living hat. About an hour later he stepped on a death adder. One of the aussie soldiers laughed and said...'Welcome to the Australian bush, Sir'.

While his men were settling in the Major found him to say that he had an urgent recall to home base leaving the Captain in charge of the whole exercise.

'All the plans are in our bivvy, you know the safe combination. Best with everything, John,.

They shook hands and the Major was away in a jeep with a driver.

'Christ, he thought, now I'll be here the whole bloody time without a shower'.

He and the Major had made planes to take turns returning to the barracks to clean up. The Captain wouldn't leave his men so they were all in for it. He joined them and the training started. The Australians did maneuvers differently relying on a lot of high tech equipment which impressed his men a lot. They stared at all the fancy laptops and phones. He knew his men were superior in hand to hand combat; they were deadly with knives, average with rifles so a lot of time would be spent on the rifle range. In the coming days they were up before first light, fed and marched to the firing range; most became proficient at it and he was proud when they all mastered the skill of the rifle grenade. In the evenings he listened to the men swapping stories; he had learned their language and in turn had tried to teach them English. He laughed when they spoke it with his brogue.

Towards the end of the training days the weather changed. The rain and storms started. They hurriedly de-camped, fleeing before the heavy rains and mud slides. After years of drought the 'big wet' hit with a force that over filled dams and sent inland seas waving across the desert.    The leaden skies shrouded the hills in mist and flocks of Magpie geese took to flight.    There were snakes everywhere and spiders the size of dinner plates were washed across the roads.    All were glad to return to the barracks.

That night the Captain cleaned up and went to the Officer's bar where he totally tiled himself.    He became maudlin and sentimental and the idea of a trip to Belfast overtook his thoughts. He had months of leave time owing so he thought...'why not'. On the return trip back to Borneo, he detoured for a few days in Cairns then back to his base.    He put the paper work in and in a fortnight he landed at Aldergrove airport.    It wasn't the place he remembered.    Ireland was now on the world's map and it was full of tourists.    He had the foresight to reserve a room in what he thought would be an average hotel.    It was all chrome and glass, shiny to the point of blinding and expensive.    His room was impressive, huge bed, writing desk, entertainment system, a chocolate bar and plastic shamrock on the pillow.    He wandered out but the streets didn't feel right.    It was proof that you couldn't go back to places you roamed as a youth.    Memories crowed you and you realized that you had lost your footing.    He got his bearings and made way to his Aunt's house which he walked by twice before he realized that it had been done over.    A new brick façade and marble steps replaced the old wooden works.    A fancy ship's bell was fastened to the side near the door and he felt idiotic ringing it.    A balding overweight man answered and the Captain explained that he wanted to see his Aunt Minnie.    The man stared at him and said,
    ' Is it Johnnie, then?'

When he answered 'yes' the man dragged him through the doorway and embraced him like a dying saint. It took the Captain a few minutes to realize that the man was his cousin Shamus. He would never have recognized him. The young Shamus had the Irish good looks of a film star, tall, lean with wavy black hair and eyes of Atlantic blue. The girls used to fight over who would get to kiss him. This bloke had the boozer's red face and beery breath, his looks were gone replaced by jowls and an overhanging gut. Even his hands had changed, now they were short, fat and stubby covered with coarse grainy hair; the nicotine stained nails had dirt under them. He kept saying...'Johnnie, Johnnie, Johnnie' like a religious litany. The Captain got right to the point and asked about his aunt.

"Now you've got to remember, Johnnie, you've been a long time going. Remember what a terror she was ? Well she still is but in a different way. We've got to have a nurse come in and feed her and change her pads. 'Ay, in one end and out the other. Here, I'll show ye'.

He followed Shamus down a corridor into a small, smelly windowless room that was a combination storage space and laundry room. An old woman lay in restraints in a wheel chair, one of the old ones with a massive wooden back and high arms with no padding. A hoist with a shower sling was pushed against a wall, nearby was a pile of clothes and towels. Shamus was saying... 'what they do is send two nurses, they wrestle her into the sling and get the hose', he pointed to a garden hose connected to the laundry tub taps, 'and they clean her up, change her pads and feed her. She's outlived her time. She should be gone. Right, Ay, Minnie'.

He leaned down and turned her face upward so she could see.

'Tis Johnnie from the other side of the globe. He's come to see ye. Ye remember him? Got himself all beat up, he did. Long time past'.

The Captain was appalled and backed out of the room, Shamus came out and said,

'Ay, it's sad. Lets go to the pub'.

As they walked Shamus explained what he did.

"Real Estate, Johnnie, Real Estate. A smart bloke like me saw it coming. I bought cheap, sold dear, made a packet. Now I only touch the fancy stuff. There's a fortune to be made'.

They entered an old dimly lit pub heavy with cigarette smoke, stale booze smells and the rank odor of men. Shamus called to the publican...'make it two'. He got two pint glasses of stout and handed one to the Captain who thought to himself---are we going to drink standing up? Stools were pushed against the wall and the Captain sat on one of them, Shamus put his coat on another and said,

'This is how it is, Johnnie, the "troubles" are over. We're all mates now. We united; now it's all of us against them. You know, the Salamais'. The Captain asked ...who the bloody hell are the Salamais'? Shamus said, 'it's the Arabs'.

While they were drinking a man came in and said something to Shamus. After he walked away Shamus asked the Captain ...'if he remembered him'?

'No'.

'Ye should, ye almost killed his old Dad, broke his legs, ye did, with a cricket bat'

The Captain turned and faced the wall. He felt that he could read his memories carved into the old wood. He refused a second drink so they walked back to the house in silence.

'I always have a kip before tea', Shamus said as he went to a recliner, got a cushion from the floor and made himself comfortable. He was asleep in a minute. The Captain went to see his aunt. He knelt down next to her and undid one of the hand restraints and took her hand in his. He was crying, for her and him. Her blanket had fallen to the floor, he covered her up and tucked it around her legs. He kissed her on the cheek and whispered to her,

'Auntie, we'll meet again in heaven'.

He could hear Shamus snoring as he took leave of the house. The dark streets sparkled with neon; there were a lot of people about but he felt isolated, like a time traveler in a dim memory, a wanderer in an unfamiliar land. Arriving at his hotel he gave the concierge his credit card and said,

'Get me a ticket, get me a plane, just get me out of here. I don't care if I have to fly over the North Pole, just let it be done'.

He checked out, at the airport he had a long wait so he went duty free shopping. He bought gifts for his ayah and her daughter, fine thin gold necklaces with heart shaped pendants set with diamond points, he also bought them the largest box of chocolates he could find. For himself he bought clothes, books, magazines and maps. He wanted to see if the world was still the place he thought it was. He wanted reassurance, he felt that he had hallucinated the visit to his aunt's house. Finally he boarded his plane and after long hours, stops and change overs he stepped off a plane into the jungle night air. He breathed it in like it was food. He felt the air coil around him like silk; he was home. He called for a driver with a car and soon was at his accommodation unit. The ayah and her daughter kept their respectful distance but they were happy to have him back. They carried his bags and when they were inside he gave them their presents. The women were speechless with wonder and delight. The pendants in their tiny velvet boxes caught the lights and sparkled into prisms. He wanted to embrace them, hug them, kiss them, tell them how happy he was to see them; that wasn't allowed so he just stood there smiling at them while in his heart he called them family.

# The Pristine Kazoo

The two dwarfs made plans to climb Castle Hill on Saturday. He organized it with what he felt was military precision. She saw it as a day out; a chance to wear the new clothes she bought last week. He made a list of requirements: drink bottles, sun block, shady hats, insect spray, ichy bite cream, flip flops and munchies. She said to add some spending money in case there was a kiosk at the top of the Hill. He put a kazoo in the bag.

It was a perfect day, one of those bright blue sky days that Townsville is famous for. A slight flowing breeze cooled their faces when they met at the bottom of the track. He was wearing clothes purchased at the army disposal store complete with cami backpack, water bottle and his uncle's old giggle hat. He had new boots so he packed band-aids in case they caused blisters. She was in denim shorts with a paisley shirt tied at midriff. Under her Bratz hat she had bunched her red hair into bushes over her ears. Her mom's make-up had been applied to cover her freckles and she borrowed her sister's imitation wayfarers. The high top Keds she was wearing were new and they were pinching her toes. The old school pac across her shoulders contained a cossie, make-up, comb and a picture of the latest rock star idol.

They held hands as they started the climb but realizing it was dangerous on the road they veered off onto the old track that meandered to the top. They played their favorite game; he the philosopher and she the arguer. Dragonflies were zooming over head as they crossed a small causeway. She stumbled over a large rock. He told her that if she had been observing the correct method of walking, toes gripping, knees rotating, hips in alignment, balancing on the balls of her feet, all in symmetry then that clumsy stumbling would not have happened.

'Go jump yourself', she said, 'if I had been watching where my feet were going then I would have missed the meteor'.

He said, 'there is no meteor'.

She replied that there was one on the night she was born but ...'I don't know what the stars were doing on the night you were born, probably they didn't come out'.

He said, 'stars don't come out. I've explained many times that stars are always there, you just don't see them in daylight'.

The path took a sharp turn and sloped to the right and they held tight to each other to keep from falling.

'I'm hungry', she said.

He stopped, opened his pac and handed her a packet of trail mix.

'I want chocolate', she said.

'I didn't pack any; this is much healthier for you, gives you energy'.

'I'm tired anyway', she said, 'need rest'.

'You can rest when we reach the little pond'.

'No, now and here'.

She sat down and wouldn't look at him.

He said, too much yin, needs more yang. Now Mao has said...'

'Mao said; said indeed. Look what it got him, stiff as a Christmas turkey. Another old man turns to dust'.

He said, 'in his time...

'His time is over, now he's going to do something worthwhile; he's going to be a tourist attraction. Think of all the money they'll make out of him'.

'It might be against their Confucius beliefs to earn too much money'.

'Don't be a fool', she said, 'they're communists'.

The path leveled as they walked to the pond; iridescent dragonflies grouped in circles above the water. Sitting down she threw pebbles into the water; both watched the ripples fan out into patterns.

'He said', 'I'm Marc Antony and you're Cleopatra'.

'I don't want to be her. I'm tired of that game; anyway they're both dead'.

He said, 'now Freud, who was a genius, said...

'Another one ! All you talk about is dead old men, you've been in the library too long. Getting money out of people by

41

listening to their dreams. Call that genius ? That's shrewdness, Germans are famous for that'.

'He was Austrian'.

'You still don't know what you're talking about'.

'I know that I want to join the army', he said. 'They've altered their criteria, lots of people who couldn't get in before now can join'.

'O wow ! three months humping packs at Bandiana. Are you ready for that ?.

'That was the old army', he said. 'The new style is high tech with lots of gizmos'.

She said, 'you still have to swim across creeks with all your gear'.

'I can do it', he said.


Two dragonflies mated over their heads.

She said, 'I think it's amazingly fantastic that in their short life span they get to do it all. Some have to wait all sorts of time and never do anything'.

He said' 'I think it's cruel that they have so short of a time. Theirs is such a ephemeral life and if they get their wings wet they loose out on everything'.

'Well they ought to watch where they're flying'.


He sat on a log and began to hum into a kazoo. The dragon-flies drifted over their heads and hung motionless in the sunlight. When he stopped they darted away in different directions.

'He said, 'that's what I enjoy about a kazoo. Pristine...

'Funny looking things', she said. 'Why don't you play an alto flute or tenor sax. You could study the violin and give concerts in music halls. That kazoo looks like its been made by someone who's mentally defective'.

Picking a daisy she began to pull off the petals until there were only two white petals left around the yellow centre.

'The big petal is me', she said. 'You're the other one'. The centre is the universe. We're the only ones here'.

He said, 'you forgot the dragonflies'.

She said, 'they're gone. It's only us'.

He helped her get up. Holding hands they walked the long way back and played chasies around a tree; before they reached the road she did a few dance steps. They left foot prints again in the dust, his were even and measured, hers were erratic where she stamped her foot in anger and in one place she trampled the daisy into the dust.

# The Saracen

In the early days of high summer he wore sunlight like a multi-hued cloak. The rays danced over him like tiny birds and he longed to strip off his clothes and be embraced by many fluttering wings. On such days he wished to cry and catch the salty tears in his mouth. He had taught himself to deny tears. Whatever the pain no moisture seeped from his eyes, the tear ducts dried like hardened Martian channels; the probes reading...once there was water here but not now'. He was proud of the ability to remain detached, remote and resolute. Wearing the Queen's uniform for his country he became one of the faceless multitude.

His eyes were like sea water changing color with the light. When walking from the burning dry tropical sun into the frosty mess air enriched with the smells of the men; sweaty uniforms, dirt encrusted boots, stale after shave, sour breath, he was in the midst of it with eyes turning from green to light blue, sometimes his eyes threw out tiny sparkles of brown, like flecks found on rocks when the ponds start to dry up. His looks were dark, black hair flecked with silver, light eyes below a natural brow line that flowed to a nose curved slightly from an injury, black down feathered his ear lobes, clean white teeth, good skin integrity marred by deep lines and covered with a heavy dark beard. He sprung from Anglo-Saxon stock but looked Celtic with a hint of the Arab. In the ninth century Muslim pirates called Saracens had plundered the Byzantine Empire, destroying cities, putting the population to the sword, enslaving the young. One was a distant ancestor and the Saracen resemblance, while blended still was evident.

He spoke softly, clearly and hated to be interrupted. He was opinionated, knowledgeable; keenly interested in the current climate of world events but personally detached, an observer on the foibles of men in government. The younger men valued his opinion, heeded his advice and enjoyed his natural masculine presence. On the weekends they bonded in drinking sessions becoming rowdy and antagonistic. When they became annoying he withdrew to his room drinking fast and solitary. He paid for it the next day with hangovers, bitterness and injuries from drunken falls. At the start of the work week he was eager for the challenge but it would distill into waiting and boredom broken up by meals in the mess. Quiet and self absorbed, if he was impatient in the waiting line it never showed. He ate with his mates but there were times when he didn't speak and preferred to be

alone.    He lived in the single men's accommodation units bur-
dened with only three keys, one for his room, one for his locker,
the third for his bike.    Army life suited him, he was fed, clothed,
housed and paid a good wage.  He enjoyed the close camaraderie
with his mates in the work hours and the alcoholic bonding sessions were a bonus.

Sometimes he would engage the civilian staff in conversation
when he signed in.    Once he showed them a fork and told them
he could bend it using his superior mental powers.    When it
didn't alter he said...'then next time'.    Flowering Plumeria trees
grew amongst the palms outside the mess and he would pick the
flowers and leave them on the desk.

He left high school early.    His parents lived in a poor house
way; no pictures on the walls, no ornaments, nothing to brighten
the days.    They suffered in the extreme summer heat and lived
miserably in the winter.    Air conditioning was unheard of and
fans were an unaffordable luxury .    Escaping from this Irish
Catholic wife-bashing neighborhood he rented a bed-sit.  There
were homos next door to him, they were more of a curiosity then
a threat.  Hindered by lack of higher education he went welding
and for enjoyment did the drive to Nimbin for dope.    Ganga
smoking ruled his life, being a white rastaman was an option to
conventional living.    He was stoned for fifteen years but still able
to function. He drifted into the army and out again.  Re-joining
he sought improvement and the need to stay free from the dope
was the motivator.    He challenged himself to be the better person he felt he could be.  The dope smoking paranoia stayed with

him. He was suspicious of people, easily hurt by careless cruelty and he was conscious of his age among the other new recruits. He was aware of his psychotic behaviour that took over his life when he drank rum. Switching to beer overcame this but it was a tame brew compared to the over proof rum he would quaff like lolly water. He kept the darker aspects of his thoughts and actions hidden from his male contemporaries.

On one of his last weekends in Townsville before the stinger season started he drove to the beach for a swim in the calm Pacific Ocean. Later sitting on the hot sand and lost in thoughts he allowed himself to reminisce on the rough surf beaches of his youth and the thrill of getting caught in the undertow and being pulled out so far that the beach disappeared and the challenge of swimming back to shore. He remembered the meager toys and the kites he flew. Now he talked to himself like an old friend, his rambling thoughts usually focused on sports. The old time boxers were his favorites, he could tell you who took the dive, who was up, what boxer was back flat on the canvas.

If asked about girlfriends he'd say...that he was keeping his options open'. Women were a mystery to him. Not having sisters gave him no points of reference. He could get women but could not hold them. An old girlfriend accused him of not being able to talk to women and he knew that to be true. They wanted things he couldn't understand: they wanted kisses, cuddles and holding hands. He refused to do any of that. Unloved as a child he grew to an adult unable to feel or show emotion. He chased sex when it was there, hit and run them and then be out of their lives. The attraction women found in his looks quickly turned to disenchantment over his behaviour; they were relieved when he left. Vague feelings of a lingering sadness stayed with them long after his departure; it felt like they could get on with their life again. The ones he got along with best were the butch tom boys. They'd go to the gym together, he liked the way they could do hundreds of bicep curls and bench press as much as he could. He considered them equals not women. They were rough, drove utes and swore like the other soldiers. He liked the butch smell that mingled with the iron greased by sweaty hands. He hated the smell of menstruating women, the fruity sickening aroma reminded him of maggots crawling through slime meat.

He shopped in the thrift stores, all his civilian clothes were second hand. A tour of duty in Dili put a large amount of money into his bank account but he refused to spend it. There was a dark thought that if he got the boot from the army he could live on that money.

On the weekends he drank himself into a dark funnel of depression emerging on Sunday night for a meal with the other live-ins. He would smell of rum and sweat, his eyes now dark with unpleasant dreams. Wearing rumpled clothes and tousled hair he looked like a child that had outgrown its adolescence. Once he was seen wearing a tee shirt over his head, two of his mates walking behind him to hold him if he fell. His drunkenness upset his Buddhist beliefs but he likened it to the Great One's period of homeless wandering; a part of him longing for the shaven head, robe and begging bowl.

For decades he had studied martial arts; absorbing the blows and kicks, honing his mind on the various philosophies and tenets of the arts. Daily training keeps him in shape. He seems slight of build but when he removes his shirt his form is taut steel and his hands can kill. When he stands nude he is the perfect statue. Now in his mid years impotency causes him to rage, he strikes out in fury at the woman he is with. He unleashes all his dark fury on her and places a threatening hand around her throat. Finally losing control he throbs into a dry climax that leaves him breathless and weak. He hates the woman and hates himself. She took a picture that shows him as a solitary figure on a hill above the Strand, fading into the blue of the water and the lighter sky, adrift like a knot of weathered wood floating among the waves.

Before his next posting to Darwin he had two weeks standdown from the army, going to his mother's house was a way out of his thoughts. He'd drink until the urge for something stronger took hold; then meet with old mates to score drugs. Nothing could save him from wanting to be stoned for eternity. Stepping into the hot, gaudy caldron of the Brisbane night he welcomed what ever was to come.

The End

# About the author

Chiesa Irwin lives in Townsville, Queensland.

www.ingramcontent.com/pod-product-compliance
Lightning Source LLC
Chambersburg PA
CBHW071226170626
46809CB00005BA/1960

* 9 7 8 0 6 4 6 5 2 2 1 6 6 *